2001–02
NBA TEAM TRACKER

An Insider's Guide to All the Teams in the NBA!

by John Hareas

SCHOLASTIC INC.

New York   Toronto   London   Auckland   Sydney
Mexico City   New Delhi   Hong Kong   Buenos Aires

To Emma and Chris,
My all-star kids.
— J.H.

PHOTO CREDITS

NBA ENTERTAINMENT PHOTOS
COVER (ALLEN): GARY DINEEN. **COVER (DUNCAN):** GLENN JAMES. **COVER (MCGRADY):** FERNANDO MEDINA. **3 (KUKOC):** JOE MURPHY. **3 (ABDUR-RAHIM); 13 (THOMAS):** SCOTT CUNNINGHAM. **3 (PETTIT); 11 (BARRY); 12 (TOMJANOVICH); 14 (MCADOO); 17 (RILEY); 25 (WALTON); 27 (GERVIN); 28 (JOHNSON); 30 (MARAVICH):** NBA PHOTO LIBRARY. **4 (PIERCE, WALKER); 5 (DAVIS) 9 (ISSEL); 15 (BRYANT); 24 (SKILES); 29 (PETERSON, WILKENS); 31 (UNSELD):** ANDREW D. BERNSTEIN. **4 (AUERBACH); 26 (ARCHIBALD):** NEIL LEIFER. **5 (MASHBURN):** GARRETT ELLWOOD. **5 (SILAS):** DICK RAPHAEL. **17 (MOURNING); 21 (SPREWELL); 30 (STOCKTON):** GLENN JAMES. **6 (MERCER, FIZER, JORDAN); 13 (MILLER); 19 (SZCZERBIAK):** BARRY GOSSAGE. **7 (MIHM):** RON TURENNE. **7 (MILLER):** DAVID L. KYLE. **7 (PRICE); 25 (WELLS); 29 (CARTER):** SAM FORENCICH. **8 (NASH, NOWITZKI):** LAYNE MURDOCH. **8 (BLACKMAN); 15 (O'NEAL):** NATHANIEL S. BUTLER. **9 (LAFRENTZ); 22 (MCGRADY); 25 (PIPPEN):** FERNANDO MEDINA. **9 (MCDYESS); 10 (DUMARS):** DON GRAYSTON. **10 (CLEAVES):** GREG SHAMUS. **10 (STACKHOUSE):** TIM DEFRISCO. **11 (HUGHES, JAMISON); 13 (ROSE); 16 (WILLIAMS); 26 (DIVAC):** ROCKY WIDNER. **12 (FRANCIS, MOBLEY):** BILL BAPTIST. **14 (BRAND); 18 (ALLEN, ROBINSON):** GARY DINEEN. **14 (ODOM); 22 (HILL); 24 (MARBURY):** ROBERT MORA. **15 (WEST); 21 (REED):** KEN REGAN. **16 (DICKERSON, REEVES):** KIM STALLKNECHT. **17 (JONES):** MARC SEROTA. **18 (LANIER):** ROBERT LEWIS. **19 (GARNETT):** DAVID SHERMAN. **19 (MITCHELL); 23 (IVERSON, MUTOMBO):** JESSE D. GARRABRANT. **20 (KIDD), 30 (HAMILTON):** NOREN TROTMAN. **20 (MARTIN):** FRANK MCGRATH. **20 (SCOTT); 21 (CAMBY); 24 (MARION); 26 (STOJAKOVIC); 28 (PAYTON):** ANDY HAYT. **22 (ARMSTRONG):** GARY BASSING. **23 (ERVING):** JERRY WACHTER. **27 (DUNCAN); 28 (LEWIS):** CHRIS COVATTA. **27 (ROBINSON):** D. CLARKE EVANS. **30 (MALONE):** NORM PERDUE. **31 (ALEXANDER):** MITCHELL LAYTON.

No part of this publication may be reproduced, stored in a retrieval system, or transmitted in any form or by any means, electronic, mechanical, photocopying, recording, or otherwise, without written permission of the publisher. For information regarding permission, write to Scholastic Inc., Attention: Permissions Department, 555 Broadway, New York, NY 10012.

The NBA and individual NBA member team identifications, photographs, and other content used on or in this publication are trademarks, copyrighted designs, and other forms of intellectual property of NBA Properties, Inc. and the respective NBA member teams and may not be used, in whole or in part, without the prior written consent of NBA Properties, Inc. All rights reserved.

ISBN 0-439-34307-0

Copyright © 2001 by NBA Properties, Inc.
All rights reserved. Published by Scholastic Inc.

SCHOLASTIC and associated logos are trademarks and/or registered trademarks of Scholastic Inc.

12 11 10 9 8 7 6 5 4 3 2   1 2 3 4 5 6/0

Printed in the U.S.A.
First Scholastic printing, December 2001
Book Design: Michael Malone

ATLANTA HAWKS

HISTORY OF TEAM NICKNAME

The Hawks were named after the Sauk Indian chief Black Hawk, who led an uprising during the early 1830s that became known as the Black Hawk War. The war was fought in an area along the Mississippi River that became home to the Tri-City Blackhawks basketball team in 1946. The team later shortened its name and moved to Milwaukee, then St. Louis, before finding a permanent place in Atlanta in 1968.

nba.com FUN FACT

Bob Pettit guided the Hawks to their only championship in 1958. The power forward was also the first player in NBA history to reach 20,000 points.

Bob Pettit

PLAYER TO WATCH

SHAREEF ABDUR-RAHIM
New Arrival

All eyes will be on Shareef this season. The 6-9 forward returns to his home state and should soar in his first season in Atlanta. Whether he's breaking his man off the dribble for a jumper or driving to the hoop, Shareef will be a magnet for opposing defenses because of his offensive skills. Look for his teammates to benefit with lots of open looks.

PLAYER TO WATCH

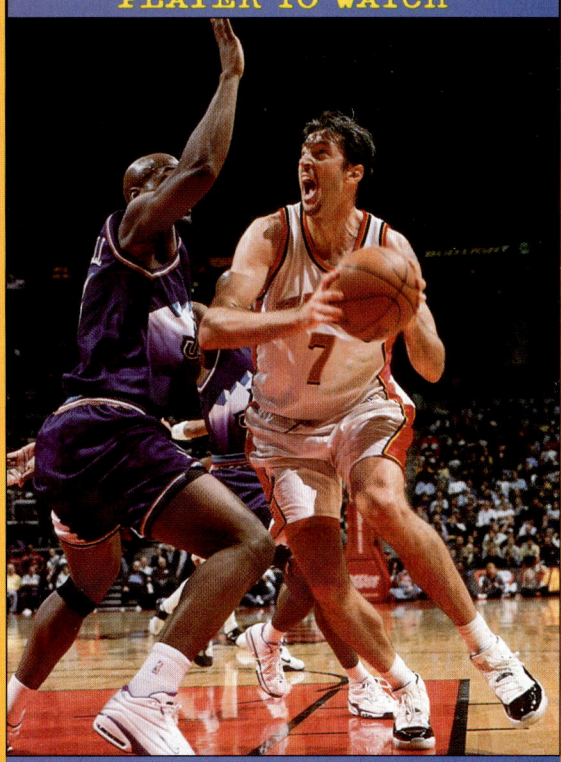

TONI KUKOC

What Toni Kukoc brings to the Hawks in his first full season in Atlanta is more than great all-around skills—it's championship leadership. The 6-11 forward won three rings as a member of the Chicago Bulls and will help guide the Hawks both on and off the court this season.

THE KUKOC FACTOR:
Team Scoring Average With and Without Toni

- 99.4 points per game (team avg.) — 17 games with Kukoc
- 88.8 points per game (team avg.) — 65 games without Kukoc

PAST PERFORMANCE

Season	W–L	Central Division	Playoff Finish
1995–96	46–36	4th (tied)	Lost in Eastern Conf. Semifinals to Orlando (1–4)
1996–97	56–26	2nd	Lost in Eastern Conf. Semifinals to Chicago (1–4)
1997–98	50–32	4th	Lost in First Round to Charlotte (1–3)
1998–99	31–19	2nd	Lost in Eastern Conf. Semifinals to New York (0–4)
1999–00	28–54	7th	Did Not Qualify
2000–01	25–57	7th	Did Not Qualify

BOSTON CELTICS

HISTORY OF TEAM NICKNAME

Can you imagine the Boston Whirlwinds or the Boston Olympians? Or how about the Boston Unicorns? Well, back in 1946, one of those names almost became a reality until team founder Walter Brown took charge. He selected Celtics, explaining, "The name has a great basketball tradition from the old original Celtics in New York (1914–1939). And Boston is full of Irishmen."

nba.com FUN FACT

Red Auerbach defined coaching greatness. He guided the Celtics to nine championships and led them to 938 regular-season wins.

Red Auerbach

PLAYER TO WATCH: PAUL PIERCE

When it comes to offense, the Celtics look no further than Paul Pierce. The 6-6 shooting guard became the first Celtic since Larry Bird to score 2,000 points and average 25.3 points per game in a season. But Pierce isn't just tough to beat on offense—he excels at defense as well.

PLAYER TO WATCH: ANTOINE WALKER

Like Paul Pierce, Antoine Walker knows how to fill the basket. Walker averaged more than 23 points per game in 2000–01 and can play multiple positions, including point guard. The 6-9 power forward is also one of the league's most tireless players—he finished second in minutes played last season.

BOSTON'S DYNAMIC DUO: Top Scoring Combos in the NBA Last Season

- **57.2 points per game (combined)** — Shaquille O'Neal and Kobe Bryant (L.A. Lakers)
- **48.7 points per game (combined)** — Antoine Walker and Paul Pierce (Boston Celtics)

PAST PERFORMANCE

Season	W–L	Atlantic Division	Playoff Finish
1995–96	33–49	5th	Did Not Qualify
1996–97	15–67	7th	Did Not Qualify
1997–98	36–46	6th	Did Not Qualify
1998–99	19–31	5th	Did Not Qualify
1999–00	35–47	5th	Did Not Qualify
2000–01	36–46	5th	Did Not Qualify

Charlotte Hornets

HISTORY OF TEAM NICKNAME

You have to go way back to the Revolutionary War to find the origin of this nickname. While leading British forces in the Carolinas, Lord Cornwallis wrote to King George III that the battle there was "like fighting in a hornet's nest." Centuries later, the team selected Hornets in a contest after fans objected to the league's original choice, the Charlotte Spirit.

nba.com FUN FACT

Charlotte Hornets' Head Coach, Paul Silas, played 16 years in the NBA and won two titles with Boston and one with Seattle.

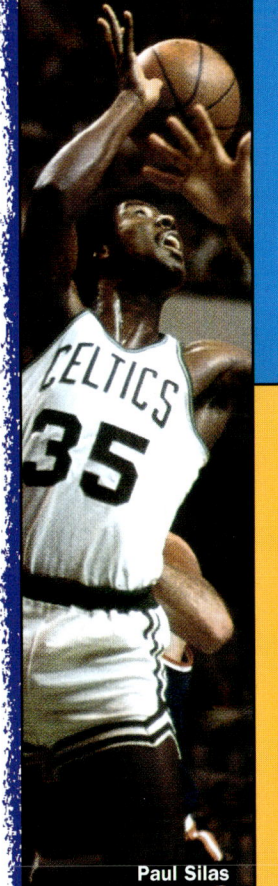

Paul Silas

PLAYER TO WATCH: BARON DAVIS

Baron Davis is emerging as one of the NBA's most exciting point guards. Last season's best-kept secret scores and rebounds in an explosive manner. Davis is a fearless player, and his opponents are becoming increasingly afraid of his game.

PLAYER TO WATCH: JAMAL MASHBURN

How good is Jamal Mashburn? He is one of only three players in the NBA who ranked in the top 30 in points, rebounds and assists last season. So if Mashburn isn't knocking down shots, he's rebounding or passing to help his team win.

BARON'S BIG JUMP: Baron Davis's Regular-Season Scoring Increase

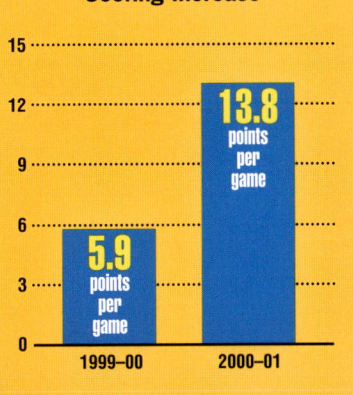

- 1999–00: 5.9 points per game
- 2000–01: 13.8 points per game

PAST PERFORMANCE

Season	W–L	Central Division	Playoff Finish
1995–96	41–41	6th	Did Not Qualify
1996–97	54–28	3rd (tied)	Lost in First Round to New York (0–3)
1997–98	51–31	3rd	Lost in Eastern Conf. Semifinals to Chicago (1–4)
1998–99	26–24	5th	Did Not Qualify
1999–00	49–33	2nd	Lost in First Round to Philadelphia (0–3)
2000–01	46–36	3rd	Lost in Eastern Conf. Semifinals to Milwaukee (0–4)

Chicago Bulls

HISTORY OF TEAM NICKNAME

In 1966, owner Richard Klein wanted his team to reflect a fighting, never-say-quit attitude. The nickname had to be bold because basketball had been a hard sell in Chicago. So what nickname did Klein choose? Bulls, of course. Given the fact the Bulls stampeded to six NBA championships in its 34-year history, Klein was certainly ahead of his time.

nba.com FUN FACT

Michael Jordan not only led Chicago to six NBA championships, he also won 10 scoring titles. He is tied with the great Wilt Chamberlain for the most scoring titles.

Michael Jordan

PLAYER TO WATCH: MARCUS FIZER

This is the season Marcus Fizer flexes his muscles at the power forward position. The second-year player will use his considerable size—6-9, 262 pounds—to grab rebounds and score points in the paint for the Bulls. Marcus will be in a prime position to improve upon last season's averages of 9.5 points and 4.3 rebounds per game.

PLAYER TO WATCH: RON MERCER

Ron Mercer provides instant offense for the Bulls. He can heat up in a hurry, whether he's running the open floor for easy baskets or burying jumpers from the perimeter. And the 6-7 shooting guard rarely takes a breather. Last season, he averaged 41.6 minutes per game. Oh, did we tell you there are 48 minutes in a game?! Whew!

RON MERCER: THE RUNNING MAN
Ron Mercer's Minutes Per Game Average

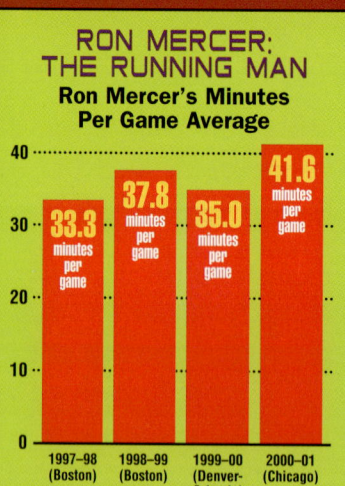

Season	Minutes per game
1997–98 (Boston)	33.3
1998–99 (Boston)	37.8
1999–00 (Denver-Orlando)	35.0
2000–01 (Chicago)	41.6

PAST PERFORMANCE

Season	W–L	Central Division	Playoff Finish
1995–96	72–10	1st	NBA Champions (Defeated Seattle, 4–2)
1996–97	69–13	1st	NBA Champions (Defeated Utah, 4–2)
1997–98	62–20	1st	NBA Champions (Defeated Utah, 4–2)
1998–99	13–37	8th	Did Not Qualify
1999–00	17–65	8th	Did Not Qualify
2000–01	15–67	8th	Did Not Qualify

CLEVELAND CAVALIERS

HISTORY OF TEAM NICKNAME

Jays. Foresters. Towers. Presidents. Those were the finalists when a Cleveland newspaper held a name-the-team contest. But more than 2,000 of the 6,000 fans who voted wanted the Cavaliers. The contest winner said, "The Cavaliers represent a group of daring, fearless men, whose life's pact was 'Never surrender, no matter what the odds.'"

nba.com FUN FACT

Former point guard Mark Price played nine seasons with the Cavaliers and is the franchise's all-time leader in assists with 4,206.

Mark Price

PLAYER TO WATCH: CHRIS MIHM

At 7-1, Chris Mihm is the anchor in the middle for the Cavaliers. The second-year player is a good shooter and rebounder who can play an up-tempo game. He's a skilled player whose rookie averages of 7.6 points per game and 4.7 rebounds per game should improve this season.

PLAYER TO WATCH: ANDRE MILLER

Andre Miller doesn't burn opponents with flash and pizzazz but with results. Big-time results. The Cavaliers' point guard hasn't missed a game in his first two seasons, and is the premier assist man in the Eastern Conference. But Miller isn't a one-trick guy—he can score with the best as well.

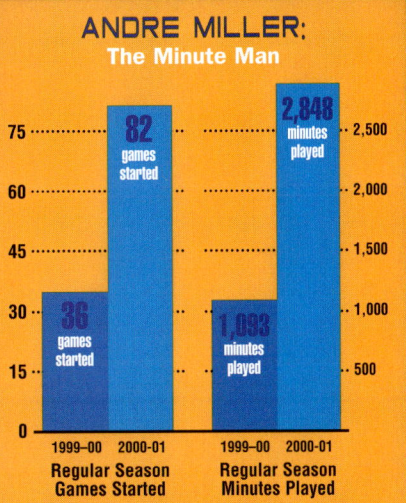

ANDRE MILLER: The Minute Man

	1999–00	2000–01
Regular Season Games Started	36	82
Regular Season Minutes Played	1,093	2,848

PAST PERFORMANCE

Season	W–L	Central Division	Playoff Finish
1995–96	47–35	3rd	Lost in First Round to New York (0–3)
1996–97	42–40	5th	Did Not Qualify
1997–98	47–35	5th	Lost in First Round to Indiana (1–3)
1998–99	22–28	7th	Did Not Qualify
1999–00	32–50	6th	Did Not Qualify
2000–01	30–52	6th	Did Not Qualify

DALLAS MAVERICKS

HISTORY OF TEAM NICKNAME

Think of Texas and you think of cowboys and wide-open spaces. That Western setting certainly wasn't forgotten when a local radio station held a contest to name the NBA expansion franchise in 1980. After considering several choices, including Wranglers and Express, the Mavericks were selected because of Texas's world-famous cowboy image.

nba.com FUN FACT

Former guard and Mavs' great Rolando Blackman is the franchise's all-time leading scorer with 16,643 points. His number, 22, is retired by the team.

PLAYER TO WATCH: STEVE NASH

Nicknamed "Captain Canada" because of his Canadian roots, Steve Nash is the man in charge of the Mavericks. Last season, the 6-3 point guard led the Mavericks to the playoffs for the first time since 1990. He's one of the game's best shooters and is emerging as one of its best point guards as well.

PLAYER TO WATCH: DIRK NOWITZKI

What can't Dirk Nowitzki do? The 7-0 German native gives opponents nightmares with his three-point shooting and his ability to block shots. Nowitzki is only the second player in NBA history to have more than 100 three-pointers and 100 blocks in the same season.

STEVE NASH: Making His Point
Steve Nash's Regular-Season Scoring Increase

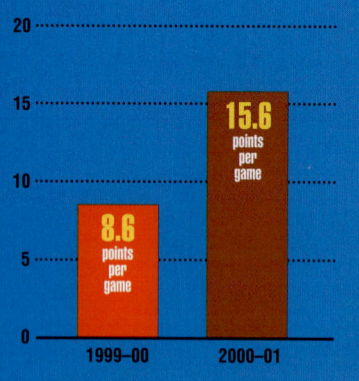

- 1999–00: 8.6 points per game
- 2000–01: 15.6 points per game

PAST PERFORMANCE

Season	W–L	Midwest Division	Playoff Finish
1995–96	26–56	5th (tied)	Did Not Qualify
1996–97	24–58	4th	Did Not Qualify
1997–98	20–62	5th	Did Not Qualify
1998–99	19–31	5th	Did Not Qualify
1999–00	40–42	4th	Did Not Qualify
2000–01	53–29	2nd (tied)	Lost in Western Conf. Semifinals to San Antonio (1–4)

Rolando Blackman

DENVER NUGGETS

HISTORY OF TEAM NICKNAME

Denver's team was originally called the Rockets when they entered the American Basketball Association in 1967, but changed their name before the 1974–75 season. Why? Because Denver was considering a move to the NBA, and the NBA already had a team by that name—the San Diego Rockets. Team officials chose Nuggets because of the 19th-century gold rush. Two years later the Denver Nuggets joined the NBA.

nba.com FUN FACT

Hall of Famer and former Nugget great Dan Issel scored 28 points in the highest-scoring game in NBA history. Denver lost to the Detroit Pistons 186–184 on December 13, 1983.

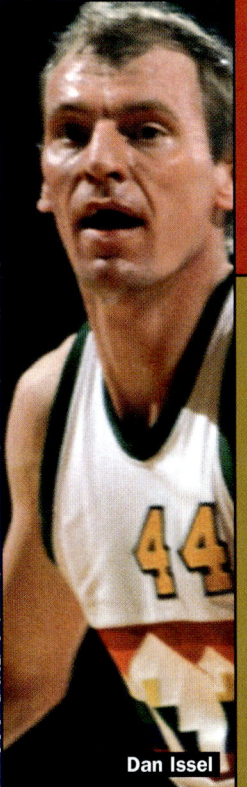

Dan Issel

PLAYER TO WATCH: RAEF LAFRENTZ

Raef LaFrentz causes matchup problems for opposing teams. Leave him open on the perimeter and the 6-11 center will bury a jump shot. Overplay him and watch him drive inside for an easy two points. LaFrentz will be the key for Denver's playoff drive this season.

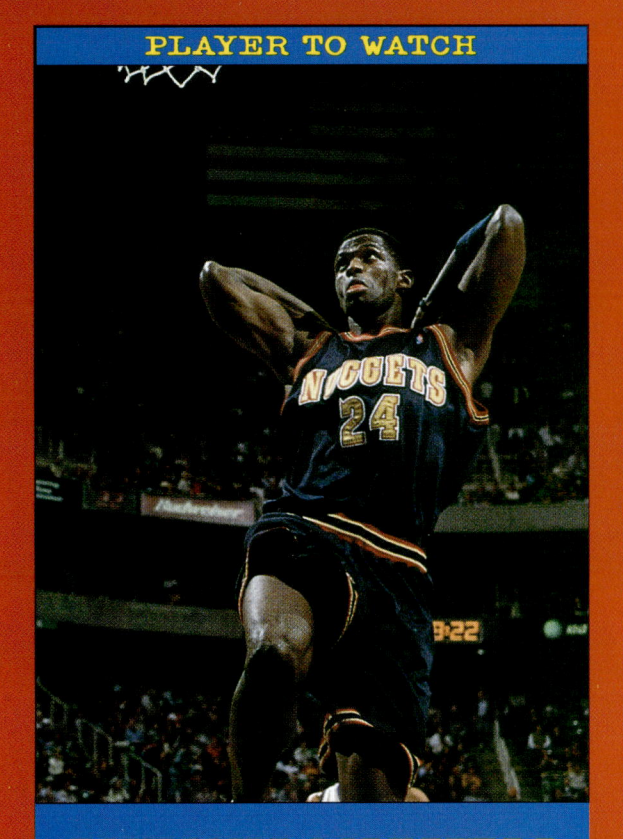

PLAYER TO WATCH: ANTONIO MCDYESS

Speed and power define Antonio McDyess's game. The 6-9 power forward is extremely active around the basket, whether he's scoring, rebounding or sending an opponent's shot into the stands. But his game doesn't merely focus around the basket—leave him open for a 15-footer and he'll make you pay.

ANTONIO McDYESS: Golden Nugget
Denver's All-Time Scoring Leaders

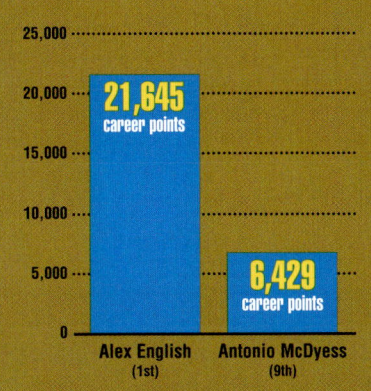

- Alex English (1st): 21,645 career points
- Antonio McDyess (9th): 6,429 career points

PAST PERFORMANCE

Season	W–L	Midwest Division	Playoff Finish
1995–96	35–47	4th	Did Not Qualify
1996–97	21–61	5th	Did Not Qualify
1997–98	11–71	7th	Did Not Qualify
1998–99	14–36	6th	Did Not Qualify
1999–00	35–47	5th	Did Not Qualify
2000–01	40–42	6th	Did Not Qualify

DETROIT PISTONS

HISTORY OF TEAM NICKNAME

Zollner Machine Works was a piston-manufacturing plant in Fort Wayne, Indiana. The company's founder, Fred Zollner, also owned a basketball team in the National Basketball League called—what else?—the Fort Wayne Zollner Pistons. When the team moved to Detroit, the automobile capital of the world, the nickname Pistons stuck because a piston is an essential part of a vehicle's engine.

nba.com FUN FACT

Joe Dumars, President of Basketball Operations for the Pistons, helped guide the franchise to two NBA championships as a player.

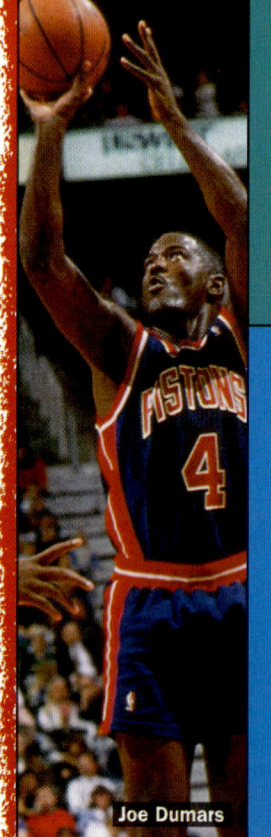

Joe Dumars

PLAYER TO WATCH: MATEEN CLEAVES

Mateen Cleaves is a local hero. Born and raised in Michigan, Cleaves was a huge success at Michigan State, where he helped lead the Spartans to a national championship. Now, in his second season, Cleaves hopes to make an additional impact with his pass first, shoot second approach to the game.

PLAYER TO WATCH: JERRY STACKHOUSE

This Piston runs on all cylinders all the time. Jerry Stackhouse had the most productive offensive season in franchise history when he averaged 29.8 points per game, second in the league. But Jerry isn't all about scoring—he ranked second among shooting guards in assists, averaging 5.1 per game.

JERRY STACKHOUSE: High-Octane Offense
Highest Detroit Single-Season Scoring Average

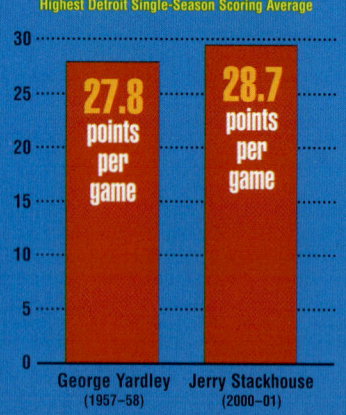

- George Yardley (1957–58): 27.8 points per game
- Jerry Stackhouse (2000–01): 28.7 points per game

PAST PERFORMANCE

Season	W–L	Central Division	Playoff Finish
1995–96	46–36	4th (tied)	Lost in First Round to Orlando (0–3)
1996–97	54–28	3rd (tied)	Lost in First Round to Atlanta (2–3)
1997–98	37–45	6th	Did Not Qualify
1998–99	29–21	3rd	Lost in First Round to Atlanta (2–3)
1999–00	42–40	4th (tied)	Lost in First Round to Miami (0–3)
2000–01	32–50	5th	Did Not Qualify

Golden State Warriors

HISTORY OF TEAM NICKNAME

As a charter member of the NBA in 1946, the Warriors started out in Philadelphia and were named after a former American Basketball League team. When the team relocated to California in 1962, they were called the San Francisco Warriors. The team later crossed the bay to Oakland and adopted California's nickname, the Golden State, which is how they became the Golden State Warriors.

nba.com FUN FACT

Rick Barry led the Warriors to one of the biggest upsets in NBA Finals history in 1975, when Golden State swept the favored Washington Bullets, 4–0.

Rick Barry

PLAYER TO WATCH: LARRY HUGHES

Creativity and versatility, that's Larry Hughes' game. Whether he's draining jumpers at either the shooting guard or small forward positions, or handling the ball at the point, Larry is always looking to make something happen. This season, the 6-5 player should once again see action at all three positions in Golden State's up-tempo attack.

PLAYER TO WATCH: ANTAWN JAMISON

What more can Antawn Jamison do? After all, last season he distinguished himself as one of the NBA's top scorers, averaging 24.9 points per game, including back-to-back 50-point games. The last player who did that was Michael Jordan. Pretty good company for Jamison, wouldn't you say?

ANTAWN'S THREE-POINT JUMP: Antawn Jamison's Three-Pointers (Made/Attempted)

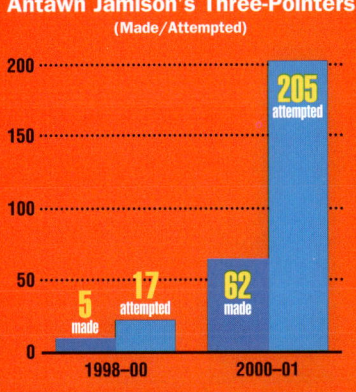

- 1998–00: 5 made, 17 attempted
- 2000–01: 62 made, 205 attempted

PAST PERFORMANCE

Season	W–L	Pacific Division	Playoff Finish
1995–96	36–46	6th	Did Not Qualify
1996–97	30–52	7th	Did Not Qualify
1997–98	19–63	6th	Did Not Qualify
1998–99	21–29	6th	Did Not Qualify
1999–00	19–63	6th	Did Not Qualify
2000–01	17–65	7th	Did Not Qualify

HOUSTON ROCKETS

HISTORY OF TEAM NICKNAME

San Diego was known as the "City in Motion" in the late 1960s. It was also home to the spacecraft manufacturer Atlas Rockets. So when the city was awarded an NBA franchise in 1967, local fans selected Rockets to reflect the city's "speedy" image. In 1971, the team moved to Houston, which is, luckily, home to the Johnson Space Center.

nba.com FUN FACT

Houston Head Coach Rudy Tomjanovich played 11 seasons for the Rockets and was a five-time All-Star.

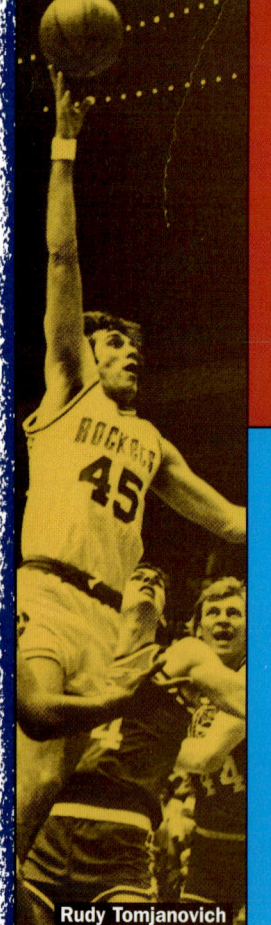

PLAYER TO WATCH: STEVE FRANCIS

Every time Steve Francis steps onto the court, opponents have to watch out for a triple-double. The explosive point guard is Houston's Mr. Everything, having led his team in points, rebounds and assists last season. And to top it all off, the 6-3 Francis led all NBA guards in rebounding as well!

PLAYER TO WATCH: CUTTINO MOBLEY

Cuttino Mobley is proving a lot of teams wrong. The 41st pick of the 1998 NBA Draft, Mobley went from sixth man to starter and is a valuable member of Houston's up-tempo offense. The 6-4 shooting guard can beat teams with his perimeter game or his ability to penetrate the defense.

HOUSTON, WE HAVE LIFTOFF
Houston's Win Total Increase

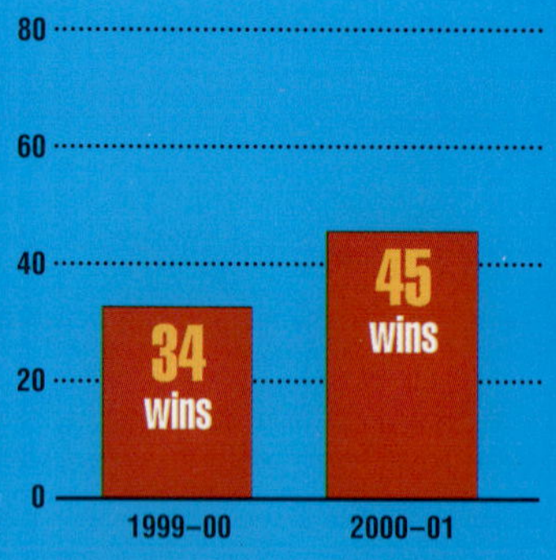

- 1999–00: 34 wins
- 2000–01: 45 wins

PAST PERFORMANCE

Season	W–L	Midwest Division	Playoff Finish
1995–96	48–34	3rd	Lost in Western Conf. Semifinals to Seattle (0–4)
1996–97	57–25	2nd	Lost in Western Conf. Finals to Utah (2–4)
1997–98	41–41	4th	Lost in First Round to Utah (2–3)
1998–99	31–19	3rd	Lost in First Round to L.A. Lakers (1–3)
1999–00	34–48	6th	Did Not Qualify
2000–01	45–37	5th	Did Not Qualify

Rudy Tomjanovich

INDIANA PACERS

HISTORY OF TEAM NICKNAME

When this former American Basketball Association team announced its nickname in 1967 at a press conference, the organization said that it hoped to set the "pace" in professional basketball. Makes sense. After all, Indiana also sets the pace in auto and horse racing. There is a "pace car" that leads the Indianapolis 500 race every year, and harness racing uses pacers as well.

nba.com FUN FACT

Pacers Head Coach and former Detroit Piston Isiah Thomas owns the NBA Finals single-game record for most points in one quarter with 25. He accomplished this in Game 6 of the 1988 NBA Finals vs. the Los Angeles Lakers.

Isiah Thomas

PLAYER TO WATCH: REGGIE MILLER

Some players live for pressure situations and an opportunity to be the hero. Reggie Miller is one of those players. Miller has earned his reputation as one of the NBA's best clutch shooters of all time. His ability to score in bunches and shoot from well behind the three-point line has become legendary.

PLAYER TO WATCH: JALEN ROSE

The scouting report on Jalen Rose is: good scorer, good rebounder, good assist man. The bottom line: good luck defending him. At 6-8, Rose has a height advantage on opposing point guards and creates all sorts of problems for defenders. So much for scouting reports.

REGGIE: Mr. High Percentage
Reggie Miller's Free-Throw Percentage

- 2000–01: .928 free-throw percentage
- Career: .884 free-throw percentage

PAST PERFORMANCE

Season	W–L	Central Division	Playoff Finish
1995–96	52–30	2nd	Lost in First Round to Atlanta (2–3)
1996–97	39–43	6th	Did Not Qualify
1997–98	58–24	2nd	Lost in Eastern Conf. Finals to Chicago (3–4)
1998–99	33–17	1st	Lost in Eastern Conf. Finals to New York (2–4)
1999–00	56–26	1st	Lost in NBA Finals to L.A. Lakers (2–4)
2000–01	41–41	4th	Lost in First Round to Philadelphia (1–3)

13

LOS ANGELES CLIPPERS

HISTORY OF TEAM NICKNAME

Some of the world's most beautiful sailboats grace the Pacific Ocean off the San Diego coast. They are descendants of great sailing ships called "clipper ships." When the Buffalo Braves relocated to San Diego in 1978, the team held a contest and more than 14,000 people voted for a new team name—Clippers. The nickname stuck when the team moved to Los Angeles in 1984.

nba.com FUN FACT

One of the best shooters of all time, Bob McAdoo, won three consecutive scoring titles as a member of the Buffalo Braves.

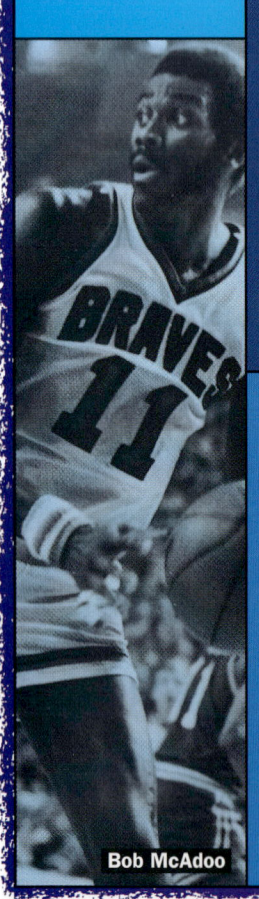

PLAYER TO WATCH
ELTON BRAND
New Arrival

What does Elton Brand bring to the Clippers? Rock-solid production. In his first two seasons with the Chicago Bulls, Elton averaged 20 points and 10 rebounds per game. Elton's ability to muscle opponents inside for points and rebounds should help open up the Clippers' perimeter game, which is bad news for their opponents.

PLAYER TO WATCH
LAMAR ODOM

Lamar Odom can score on anyone. Or pass on anyone. This 6-10 forward is extremely versatile. He can run an offense or score underneath the basket. It's always up to him, not the defender. Lamar is looking to lead the young Clippers to their first playoff berth since 1997.

CLIPPERS SET SAIL: L.A.'s Win Increase

- 1999–00: 15 wins
- 2000–01: 31 wins

PAST PERFORMANCE

Season	W–L	Pacific Division	Playoff Finish
1995–96	29–53	7th	Did Not Qualify
1996–97	36–46	5th	Lost in First Round to Utah (0–3)
1997–98	17–65	7th	Did Not Qualify
1998–99	9–41	7th	Did Not Qualify
1999–00	15–67	7th	Did Not Qualify
2000–01	31–51	6th	Did Not Qualify

Bob McAdoo

14

Los Angeles Lakers

HISTORY OF TEAM NICKNAME

Since the Minnesota State motto is "The Land of 10,000 Lakes," it is only fitting that the basketball team that started out there be called the Lakers. The Lakers eventually became the NBA's first dynasty. When the franchise moved to Los Angeles in 1960, the nickname stuck and the team's success also followed. The Los Angeles Lakers became the NBA's third dynasty, winning five titles during the 1980s.

nba.com FUN FACT

Nicknamed "Mr. Clutch" for his ability to come through in pressure situations, Jerry West starred for the Lakers and was the third player in NBA history to reach 25,000 points.

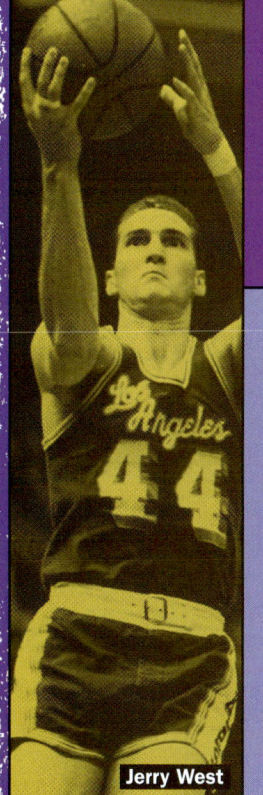

Jerry West

PLAYER TO WATCH: KOBE BRYANT

At age 23, Kobe Bryant has already established himself as one of the game's best all-around guards. Offensively, he can slash to the hoop or knock down jumper after jumper. Defensively, he can shut down an opponent with tough defense. And did we mention that he's only 23?

PLAYER TO WATCH: SHAQUILLE O'NEAL

Shaquille O'Neal is an unstoppable force. No one can guard Shaq alone, and it usually takes two or three players just to slow him down. At 7-1 and 305 pounds, Shaq scores and rebounds at will. It won't be any different this season as the Diesel sets his sights on another championship ring.

KOBE: Climbing the Scoring Ladder
Kobe Bryant's Regular-Season Scoring Increases

Season	Points per game
1996–97	7.6
1997–98	15.4
1998–99	19.9
1999–00	22.5
2000–01	28.5

PAST PERFORMANCE

Season	W–L	Pacific Division	Playoff Finish
1995–96	53–29	2nd	Lost in First Round to Houston (1–3)
1996–97	56–26	2nd	Lost in Western Conf. Semifinals to Utah (1–4)
1997–98	61–21	1st (tied)	Lost in Western Conf. Finals to Utah (0–4)
1998–99	31–19	2nd	Lost in Western Conf. Semifinals to San Antonio (0–4)
1999–00	67–15	1st	NBA Champions (Defeated Indiana, 4–2)
2000–01	56–26	1st	NBA Champions (Defeated Philadelphia, 4–1)

45

Memphis Grizzlies

HISTORY OF TEAM NICKNAME

After six seasons in Vancouver, the Grizzlies moved to Memphis for the 2001-02 season. The team retained their original nickname, which is derived from its former home, Vancouver, British Columbia, which is home to 20,000 grizzly bears.

nba.com FUN FACT

Bryant Reeves was the first collegian to be picked by the Grizzlies. The sixth pick of the 1995 NBA Draft, Reeves averaged 13.3 points in his rookie season.

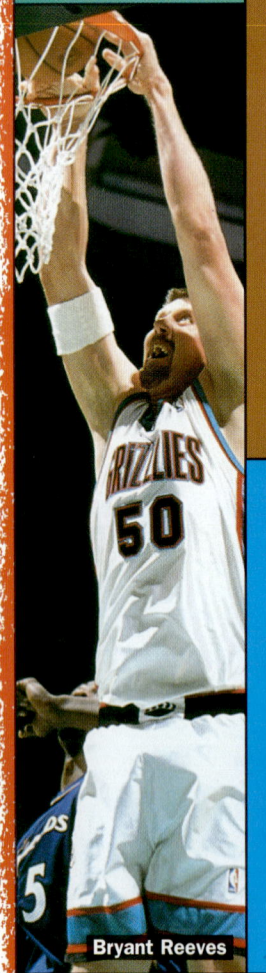

PLAYER TO WATCH: MICHAEL DICKERSON

Michael Dickerson's time is now. After a busy offseason filled with player transactions for the Grizzlies, Dickerson should be the focal point of the team's up-tempo offense. The 6-5 guard has an inside-out game that keeps opponents off balance, and he is in position to beat his regular-season career high average of 18.2 points.

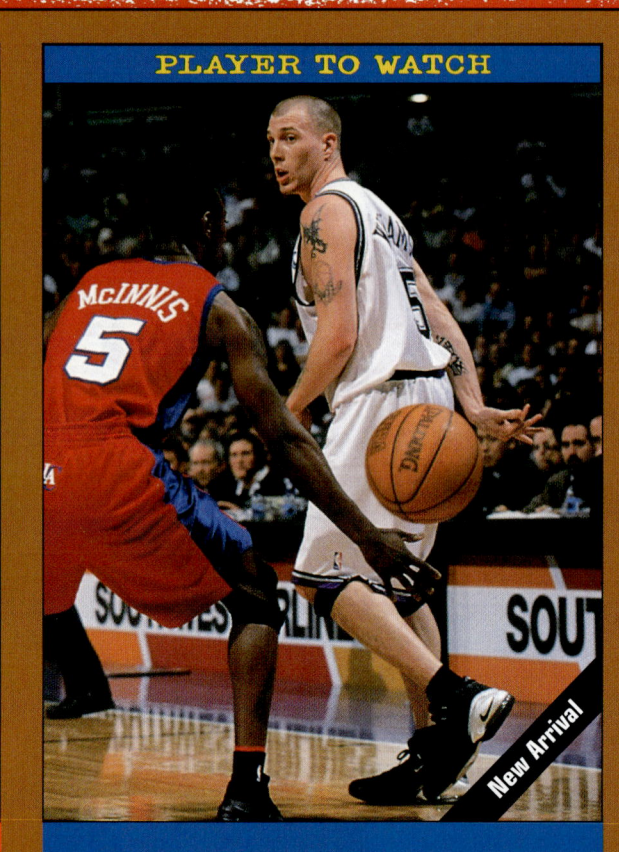

PLAYER TO WATCH: JASON WILLIAMS (New Arrival)

Whether it's jaw-dropping behind-the-back passes, ultra-quick crossover dribbles or clutch three-pointers from Graceland, Jason Williams loves to perform. Williams' uncanny ability to see the open floor should keep his Memphis teammates on their toes and happy, as they'll be on the receiving end of plenty of J-Will specials this season.

RAINING THREES: Michael Dickerson's Three-Point Touch

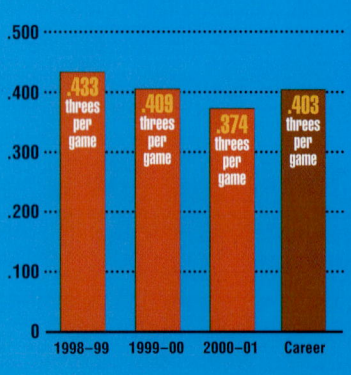

Season	Threes per game
1998–99	.433
1999–00	.409
2000–01	.374
Career	.403

PAST PERFORMANCE

Season	W–L	Midwest Division	Playoff Finish
1995–96	15–67	7th	Did Not Qualify
1996–97	14–68	7th	Did Not Qualify
1997–98	19–63	6th	Did Not Qualify
1998–99	8–42	7th	Did Not Qualify
1999–00	22–60	7th	Did Not Qualify
2000–01	23–59	7th	Did Not Qualify

Bryant Reeves

MIAMI HEAT

HISTORY OF TEAM NICKNAME

If you visit Miami, you can't help but marvel at the beaches, palm trees and flamingos. Those area symbols—along with Barracudas, Sharks, Heat, Suntan, Shade, Tornadoes, Wave and Floridians— were among the names considered when a name-the-team contest was held in 1988. More than 20,000 entries were submitted, and Heat rose to the top.

nba.com FUN FACT

Miami Head Coach Pat Riley was a member of the 1971–72 Los Angeles Lakers that won a record 33 consecutive games. That team went on to post a then-NBA best 69–13 record on its way to winning the championship.

Pat Riley

PLAYER TO WATCH: EDDIE JONES

Electrifying. That's Eddie Jones's game. The 6-7 guard mesmerizes opponents on both ends of the court. Sometimes Eddie will strip the ball on the defensive end and, in a burst of speed, drive to the other basket for an easy two or knock down a three-pointer. Either way, he won't be denied.

PLAYER TO WATCH: ALONZO MOURNING

The heart and soul of the Heat is back. Alonzo Mourning missed the majority of the 2000–01 season due to a kidney illness but aims to dominate for an entire 82-game season. Whether he is blocking shots or throwing down dunks, Zo has one goal in mind: the NBA championship.

PAT RILEY: COACHING LEGEND
All-Time Coaching Wins
Regular Season

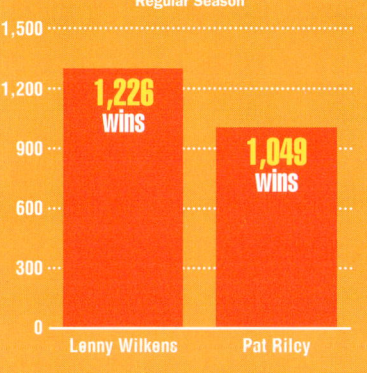

- Lenny Wilkens: 1,226 wins
- Pat Riley: 1,049 wins

PAST PERFORMANCE

Season	W–L	Atlantic Division	Playoff Finish
1995–96	42–40	3rd	Lost in First Round to Chicago (0–3)
1996–97	61–21	1st	Lost in Eastern Conf. Finals to Chicago (1–4)
1997–98	55–27	1st	Lost in First Round to New York (2–3)
1998–99	33–17	1st (tied)	Lost in First Round to New York (2–3)
1999–00	52–30	1st	Lost in Eastern Conf. Semifinals to New York (3–4)
2000–01	50–32	2nd	Lost in First Round to Charlotte (0–3)

17

Milwaukee Bucks

HISTORY OF TEAM NICKNAME

Submit the winning nickname and win a car. That's what happened when a Wisconsin resident suggested Bucks in a pool of more than 14,000 contest entries. "Bucks are spirited, good jumpers, fast and agile," said the winner. Some of the other nickname suggestions from fans included Skunks, Beavers, Hornets and Ponies—which all represent the wildlife found in Wisconsin.

nba.com FUN FACT

One of the greatest big men ever to play the game, Bob Lanier scored more than 19,000 points over the course of his 14-year career with Detroit and Milwaukee. Lanier is now scoring points off the court as the NBA's Read to Achieve spokesman.

Bob Lanier

PLAYER TO WATCH: RAY ALLEN

Ray Allen is Mr. Automatic. Leave him open on the perimeter and—*boom!*—an automatic two points. Leave him open beyond the three-point arc and...well, you get the idea. Bottom line: Watching one of Ray's shots rotate in the air before snapping the net is one of the game's prettiest sights.

PLAYER TO WATCH: GLENN ROBINSON

Glenn Robinson's nickname is "Big Dog," and how appropriate. After all, Robinson has been taking a bite out of the competition ever since he entered the league in 1994. One of the purest scorers in the game, Robinson can erase any point deficit and turn it into a Bucks' lead in a snap.

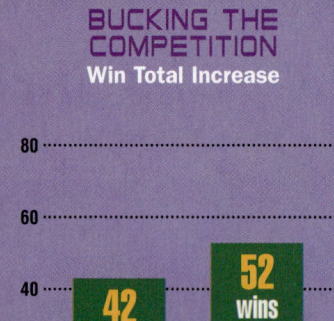

BUCKING THE COMPETITION
Win Total Increase

- 1999–00: 42 wins
- 2000–01: 52 wins

PAST PERFORMANCE

Season	W–L	Central Division	Playoff Finish
1995–96	25–57	7th	Did Not Qualify
1996–97	33–49	7th	Did Not Qualify
1997–98	36–46	7th	Did Not Qualify
1998–99	28–22	4th	Lost in First Round to Indiana (0–3)
1999–00	42–40	4th (tied)	Lost in First Round to Indiana (2–3)
2000–01	52–30	1st	Lost in Eastern Conf. Finals to Philadelphia (3–4)

MINNESOTA TIMBERWOLVES

HISTORY OF TEAM NICKNAME

Twenty-eight years after the Lakers headed to California from Minneapolis, the city welcomed a new NBA team. The date was September 17, 1988, and, even though the team wouldn't play for another year, it had a nickname. More than 6,000 fans submitted suggestions and it came down to two choices: Polars or Timberwolves. In a statewide City Council vote, the rare breed of wolf defeated Polars by a 2-to-1 margin.

nba.com FUN FACT

On November 3, 1989, forward Sam Mitchell scored the first points in Timberwolves' history when he made two free throws against the Seattle SuperSonics with 11:15 to go in the first quarter.

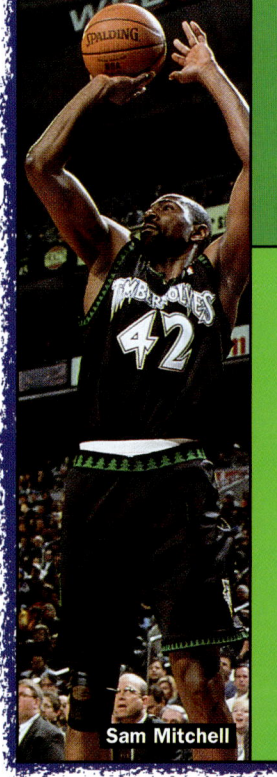

Sam Mitchell

PLAYER TO WATCH: KEVIN GARNETT

You'll be hard-pressed to find a more versatile player in the NBA than Kevin Garnett. He can score, rebound and pass with the best of them and he's 6-11! He's the leader of the Timberwolves, an All-Star, an Olympic gold medalist and he's revolutionizing the power forward position.

PLAYER TO WATCH: WALLY SZCZERBIAK

Wally's World exists on the perimeter, where he has become one of the game's best shooters. In only his third season, Szczerbiak already ranks among the league's leaders in shooting percentage. He makes half his shots! But Szczerbiak is doubly dangerous because he can also slash to the basket. Yikes!

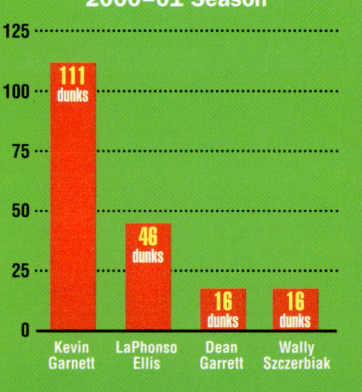

DUNK YOU VERY MUCH, KG
Dunk Totals for the 2000–01 Season

- Kevin Garnett: 111 dunks
- LaPhonso Ellis: 46 dunks
- Dean Garrett: 16 dunks
- Wally Szczerbiak: 16 dunks

PAST PERFORMANCE

Season	W–L	Midwest Division	Playoff Finish
1995-96	26–56	5th (tied)	Did Not Qualify
1996-97	40–42	3rd	Lost in First Round to Houston (0–3)
1997-98	45–37	3rd	Lost in First Round to Seattle (2–3)
1998-99	25–25	4th	Lost in First Round to San Antonio (1–3)
1999-00	50–32	3rd	Lost in First Round to Portland (1–3)
2000-01	47–35	4th	Lost in First Round to San Antonio (1–3)

NEW JERSEY NETS

HISTORY OF TEAM NICKNAME

The New Jersey Americans only lasted one season in the American Basketball Association. The next year they became the New York Nets. Why Nets? Because one of the most important parts of a basketball game is the net. Plus, Nets rhymed with the other New York pro sports franchises— Mets and Jets. The Nets joined the NBA in 1976, and one year later they moved across the Hudson River to New Jersey.

nba.com FUN FACT

New Jersey Head Coach Byron Scott played 14 seasons in the NBA, 11 with the Los Angeles Lakers where he won three championship rings.

Byron Scott

PLAYER TO WATCH
JASON KIDD
New Arrival

Who is the active leader in triple-doubles in the NBA? Who has led the league in assists for the last three seasons? And who is quite possibly the best all-around point guard in the NBA? Jason Kidd. The 6-4 All-Star now brings his basketball talents to New Jersey where he will lead the Nets in offensive wizardry.

PLAYER TO WATCH
KENYON MARTIN

When opposing players meet Kenyon Martin, they're often met with rejection. That's because the second-year small forward enjoys blocking shots when he's not rebounding or scoring. And last season, Martin became the first rookie in Nets history to record a triple-double.

DISHING THE ROCK
Kidd Joins Exclusive Group
Top Assists Leaders in Consecutive Seasons

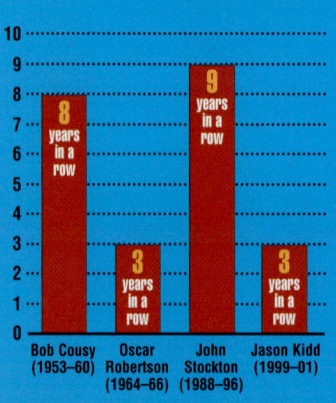

- Bob Cousy (1953–60): 8 years in a row
- Oscar Robertson (1964–66): 3 years in a row
- John Stockton (1988–96): 9 years in a row
- Jason Kidd (1999–01): 3 years in a row

PAST PERFORMANCE

Season	W–L	Atlantic Division	Playoff Finish
1995–96	30–52	6th	Did Not Qualify
1996–97	26–56	5th	Did Not Qualify
1997–98	43–39	2nd (tied)	Lost in First Round to Chicago (0–3)
1998–99	16–34	7th	Did Not Qualify
1999–00	31–51	6th	Did Not Qualify
2000–01	26–56	6th	Did Not Qualify

New York Knicks

History of Team Nickname

New York's nickname may be the most fashionable in the NBA. The term "Knickerbockers" refers to the style of pants worn by Dutch colonists who settled what is now known as New York during the 1600s. The pants, which are also known as knickers, were rolled up to just below the knee.

nba.com Fun Fact

Willis Reed became the first player in NBA history to win the regular-season MVP, All-Star Game MVP and Finals MVP in the same season. He accomplished this in the 1969–70 season.

Willis Reed

PLAYER TO WATCH
MARCUS CAMBY

Ask Marcus Camby what he prefers doing, blocking a shot or dunking a ball, and he'll say both. He'll reject an opponent's shot, leading to a Knicks' fast break, and then before you know it, he's on the receiving end to dunk for an easy two. That is Marcus's game—high energy with big results.

PLAYER TO WATCH
LATRELL SPREWELL

Latrell Sprewell is a big-game player. The bigger the game, the greater the performance. All great players are like that. His ability to score points with a variety of offensive moves has been critical to New York's success. And here's the best-kept secret: He's an underrated defender.

D·FENSE! D·FENSE!
New York's Tough Defense

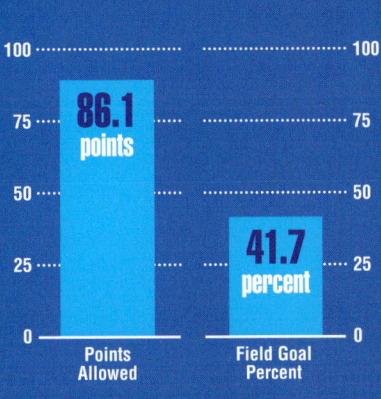

- 86.1 points — Points Allowed
- 41.7 percent — Field Goal Percent

PAST PERFORMANCE

Season	W–L	Atlantic Division	Playoff Finish
1995–96	47–35	2nd	Lost in Eastern Conf. Semifinals to Chicago (1–4)
1996–97	57–25	2nd	Lost in Eastern Conf. Semifinals to Miami (3–4)
1997–98	43–39	2nd (tied)	Lost in Eastern Conf. Semifinals to Indiana (1–4)
1998–99	27–23	4th	Lost in NBA Finals to San Antonio (1–4)
1999–00	50–32	2nd	Lost in Eastern Conf. Finals to Indiana (2–4)
2000–01	48–34	3rd	Lost in First Round to Toronto (2–3)

ORLANDO MAGIC

HISTORY OF TEAM NICKNAME

When an Orlando newspaper held a contest to select a nickname, 4,296 entries were submitted. The massive list of names, which included Heat and Tropics, was narrowed down to two: Juice and Magic. Even though Juice fit with Florida's orange and grapefruit groves, Magic was chosen because it tied in with Orlando's tourism slogan at the time, "Come to the Magic."

nba.com FUN FACT

Guard Darrell Armstrong became the first player to capture both the Sixth Man Award and the Most Improved Player Award in the same season. He received both honors after the 1998-99 season.

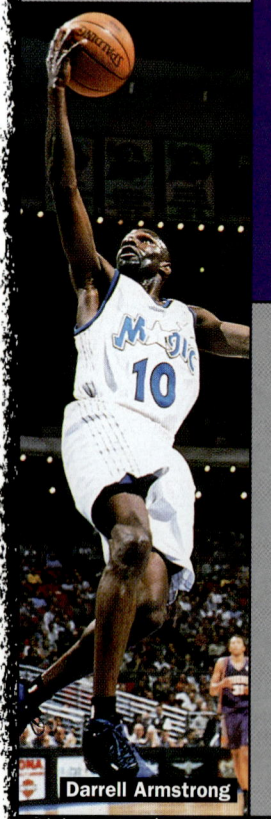

PLAYER TO WATCH: GRANT HILL

Expectations are high for Grant Hill this season. After missing most of last season, the 6-8 All-Star is anxious to show off his all-around talents. Look for Hill to run Orlando's offense. And look for Hill and Tracy McGrady to lead one of the NBA's most lethal and entertaining one-two punches.

PLAYER TO WATCH: TRACY McGRADY

Last season was truly magical for Tracy McGrady. In his first season in Orlando, the 6-8 forward blossomed into a superstar. T-Mac can do it all: score from the perimeter, slash to the basket, play defense and he's only 21 years old! What will he do for an encore this season? You'll have to watch The Magic Show to find out.

T-MAC IS TREMENDOUS
T-Mac's Regular-Season Scoring Increase

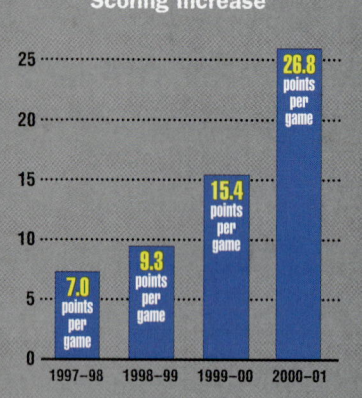

- 1997-98: 7.0 points per game
- 1998-99: 9.3 points per game
- 1999-00: 15.4 points per game
- 2000-01: 26.8 points per game

PAST PERFORMANCE

Season	W–L	Atlantic Division	Playoff Finish
1995–96	60–22	1st	Lost in Eastern Conf. Finals to Chicago (4–0)
1996–97	45–37	3rd	Lost in First Round to Miami (2–3)
1997–98	41–41	5th	Did Not Qualify
1998–99	33–17	1st (tied)	Lost in First Round to Philadelphia (1–3)
1999–00	41–41	4th	Did Not Qualify
2000–01	43–39	4th	Lost in First Round to Milwaukee (1–3)

Darrell Armstrong

PHILADELPHIA 76ERS

HISTORY OF TEAM NICKNAME

This is a team the Founding Fathers would cheer. When the Syracuse Nationals were purchased in 1963, they moved to Philadelphia. The new owners wanted a nickname that fit in the team's new home. A contest was held, and soon the Nationals became the 76ers. The new team name paid tribute to the signing of the Declaration of Independence in Philadelphia on July 4, 1776.

nba.com FUN FACT

Julius Erving was one of the greatest players ever to play in the NBA. The nine-time All-Star helped guide the Sixers to the 1983 NBA championship.

Julius Erving

PLAYER TO WATCH: ALLEN IVERSON

It is virtually impossible to guard Allen Iverson one-on-one. Just ask any NBA defender. The 6-0 guard is a human blur with his speed and wicked crossover dribble. The Philly scoring machine not only led the NBA in scoring last season, but also in steals per game. No wonder he was the 2000–01 NBA MVP.

PLAYER TO WATCH: DIKEMBE MUTOMBO

What Allen Iverson is to offense, Dikembe Mutombo is to defense. Unstoppable. The four-time NBA Defensive Player of the Year is a shot-blocking and rebounding machine who can also score. But when it comes to defense, opposing players know better than to enter the House of Mutombo because they'll be greeted with a rude welcome. Swat!

ALLEN IVERSON: NBA Scoring Champ
Allen Iverson's Regular-Season Scoring Averages

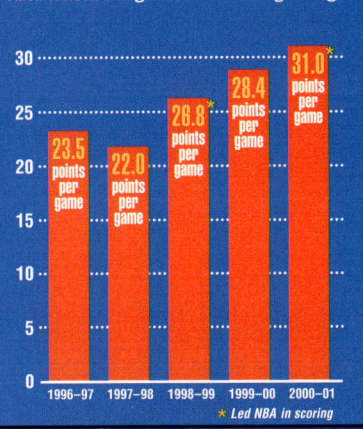

- 1996-97: 23.5 points per game
- 1997-98: 22.0 points per game
- 1998-99: 26.8 points per game
- 1999-00: 28.4 points per game
- 2000-01: 31.0 points per game *

* Led NBA in scoring

PAST PERFORMANCE

Season	W-L	Atlantic Division	Playoff Finish
1995–96	18–64	7th	Did Not Qualify
1996–97	22–60	6th	Did Not Qualify
1997–98	31–51	7th	Did Not Qualify
1998–99	28–22	3rd	Lost in Eastern Conf. Semifinals to Indiana (0–4)
1999–00	49–33	3rd	Lost in Eastern Conf. Semifinals to Indiana (2–4)
2000–01	55–26	1st	Lost in NBA Finals to L.A. Lakers (1–4)

PHOENIX SUNS

HISTORY OF TEAM NICKNAME

When the city of Phoenix was granted an NBA franchise in 1968, the team held a nickname contest and received more than 28,000 entries. Some of the more popular names included Rattlers, Tumbleweeds and Scorpions. The most popular name was Suns, which was submitted by several fans. A drawing was held, and Suns was chosen as the official nickname of the new team.

nba.com FUN FACT

Phoenix Head Coach Scott Skiles owns the NBA single-game assist record. He dished out 30 assists in a regular-season game against the Denver Nuggets on December 30, 1990. The former point guard accomplished this feat as a member of the Orlando Magic.

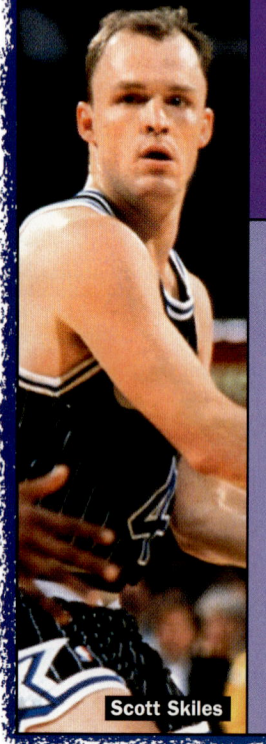

Scott Skiles

PLAYER TO WATCH
STEPHON MARBURY

The "S" in Stephon also stands for Starbury and for good reason. The sensational Suns' guard can break down an opponent with his fascinating dribbling skills or knock down a three-pointer in the blink of an eye. Look for Starbury to sizzle in his first season in the Valley of the Sun.

PLAYER TO WATCH
SHAWN MARION

His nickname is "The Matrix." If you watch Shawn Marion play, you'll know why. The 6-7 forward is one of the NBA's most athletic players, known for his acrobatic leaps and dunks, as if he's playing in 3-D! But Shawn is more than a dunker—he's a good mid-range shooter and one of the NBA's top rebounders.

SHAWN MARION: Rising Star
Shawn Marion's Regular-Season Scoring Increase

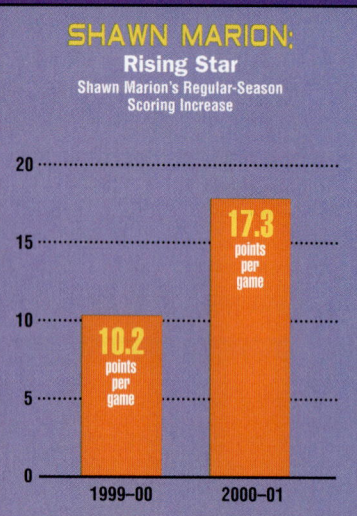

- 1999–00: 10.2 points per game
- 2000–01: 17.3 points per game

PAST PERFORMANCE

Season	W–L	Pacific Division	Playoff Finish
1995–96	41–41	4th	Lost in First Round to San Antonio (1–3)
1996–97	40–42	4th	Lost in First Round to Seattle (2–3)
1997–98	56–26	3rd	Lost in First Round to San Antonio (1–3)
1998–99	27–23	3rd (tied)	Lost in First Round to Portland (0–3)
1999–00	53–29	3rd	Lost in Western Conf. Semifinals to L.A. Lakers (1–4)
2000–01	51–31	3rd	Lost in First Round to Sacramento (1–3)

PORTLAND TRAIL BLAZERS

HISTORY OF TEAM NICKNAME

During the 1800s, many Americans took the Oregon Trail as they headed west. These pioneers traveled with horses and covered wagons. When the city of Portland was granted an expansion franchise in 1970, a contest was held to choose a nickname. The winner: Trail Blazers. "We feel Trail Blazers reflects . . . the ruggedness of the Pacific Northwest," said team founder Harry Glickman.

nba.com FUN FACT

One of the 50 Greatest Players in NBA history, Bill Walton led Portland to its only title when the Blazers defeated the Philadelpia 76ers in the 1977 NBA Finals. "Big Red" was the MVP of that series.

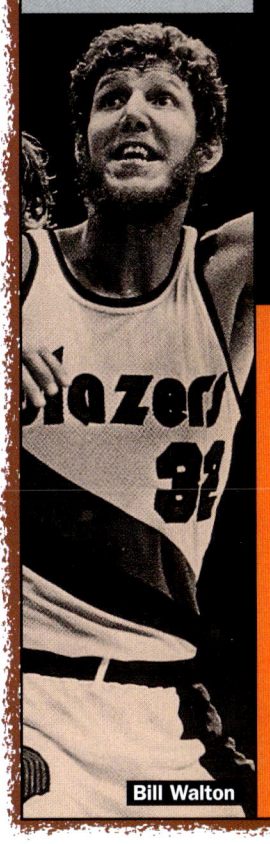

Bill Walton

PLAYER TO WATCH: SCOTTIE PIPPEN

Scottie Pippen is a coach's dream. The 6-7 small forward can fill several positions on the court. Need him to play point guard? No problem. Ask him to score like a shooting guard and he'll do it. How about grabbing rebounds against power forwards or centers? Pippen will clean the glass.

PLAYER TO WATCH: BONZI WELLS

Bonzi Wells enjoyed a breakout season in 2000–01 and emerged as one of the top players on a team full of stars. The 6-8 guard is one of the Blazers' best inside scorers and is relentless around the basket. Bonzi suffered a knee injury at the end of last season but should bounce back this season.

BIG-TIME BONZI
Bonzi Wells' Regular-Season Scoring Increases

- 1998–99: 4.4 points per game
- 1999–00: 8.8 points per game
- 2000–01: 12.7 points per game

PAST PERFORMANCE

Season	W–L	Pacific Division	Playoff Finish
1995–96	44–38	3rd	Lost in First Round to Utah (2–3)
1996–97	49–33	3rd	Lost in First Round to L.A. Lakers (1–3)
1997–98	46–36	4th	Lost in First Round to L.A. Lakers (1–3)
1998–99	35–15	1st	Lost in Western Conf. Finals to San Antonio (0–4)
1999–00	59–23	2nd	Lost in Western Conf. Finals to L.A. Lakers (3–4)
2000–01	50–32	4th	Lost in First Round to L.A. Lakers (0–3)

SACRAMENTO KINGS

HISTORY OF TEAM NICKNAME

The Rochester Royals began play in 1945 as a charter member of the National Basketball League. After joining the NBA, the franchise relocated to Cincinnati before becoming the Kansas City/Omaha Kings in 1972. Since KC was already home to a Major League Baseball team called the Royals, local fans helped select a new name—the Kings. In 1985, the team was on the move again, leaving Kansas City for Sacramento.

nba.com FUN FACT

At 6-1, Nate "Tiny" Archibald stood tall next to his opponents. He is the only player in NBA history to lead the league in scoring and assists in the same season (1972–73).

"Tiny" Archibald

PLAYER TO WATCH: VLADE DIVAC

Vlade Divac is one of the NBA's most versatile centers. He is an excellent passer who grabs rebounds and shoots the ball with a guard's touch. All of these skills, along with his leadership and ability to run the floor, have helped Divac propel the Kings to elite status.

PLAYER TO WATCH: PEJA STOJAKOVIC

Peja Stojakovic is one of the best all-around shooters in the NBA. He can drain 15-foot shots that are always met with the same results: *Swish. Swish.* What's even worse for defenders is Peja's quick release. When he catches the ball, it's in flight before they can even react.

ROYAL HIGHNESS
Sacramento Win Total Increase

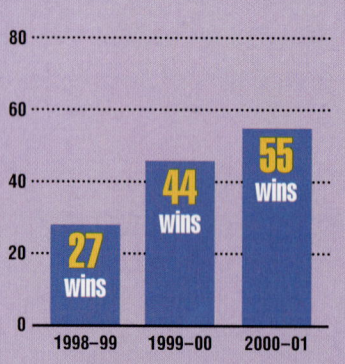

- 1998–99: 27 wins
- 1999–00: 44 wins
- 2000–01: 55 wins

PAST PERFORMANCE

Season	W–L	Pacific Division	Playoff Finish
1995–96	39–43	5th	Lost in First Round to Seattle (1–3)
1996–97	34–48	6th	Did Not Qualify
1997–98	27–55	5th	Did Not Qualify
1998–99	27–23	3rd (tied)	Lost in First Round to Utah (2–3)
1999–00	44–38	5th	Lost in First Round to L.A. Lakers (2–3)
2000–01	55–27	2nd	Lost in Western Conf. Semifinals to L.A. Lakers (0–4)

SAN ANTONIO SPURS

HISTORY OF TEAM NICKNAME

Before they were the Spurs, they were the Dallas Chaparrals of the American Basketball Association. When the team was sold to a group of San Antonio investors in 1973, the team moved to the Alamo City and was renamed Spurs in a contest. Other nickname entries included Stampede, Texans, Armadillos and Defenders. Out of all of these nicknames, the team owners thought Spurs best reflected the state's Western heritage.

nba.com FUN FACT

Hall of Famer George "Iceman" Gervin became the first guard in NBA history to win three consecutive scoring titles.

George Gervin

PLAYER TO WATCH

TIM DUNCAN

Tim Duncan is Mr. Double-Double. The 7-foot forward, who averaged 22 points and 12 rebounds per game, recorded double figures in points and rebounds in 66 games during the 2000–01 season, the most in the NBA. It's a feat he has accomplished three times in his first four seasons.

PLAYER TO WATCH

DAVID ROBINSON

David Robinson, nicknamed the Admiral, may be the most decorated serviceman ever. Check out these honors: Rookie of the Year, regular season MVP, Defensive Player of the Year, scoring title, rebounding title, blocks title and, most important, an NBA championship. It appears the Admiral may be setting sail for the Hall of Fame.

MR. DUNCAN IS MR. DOUBLE-DOUBLE
Tim Duncan's Regular-Season Scoring and Rebounding

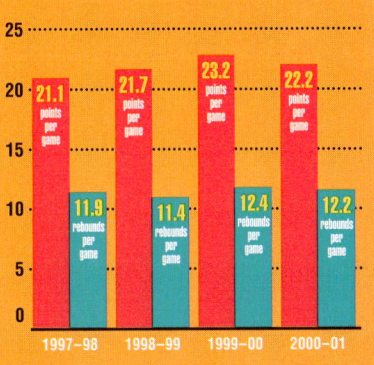

Season	Points per game	Rebounds per game
1997–98	21.1	11.9
1998–99	21.7	11.4
1999–00	23.2	12.4
2000–01	22.2	12.2

PAST PERFORMANCE

Season	W–L	Midwest Division	Playoff Finish
1995–96	59–23	1st	Lost in Western Conf. Semifinals to Utah (2–4)
1996–97	20–62	6th	Did Not Qualify
1997–98	56–26	2nd	Lost in Western Conf. Semifinals to Utah (1–4)
1998–99	37–13	1st	NBA Champions (Defeated New York, 4–1)
1999–00	53–29	2nd	Lost in First Round to Phoenix (1–3)
2000–01	58–24	1st	Lost in Western Conf. Finals to L.A. Lakers (0–4)

SEATTLE SUPERSONICS

HISTORY OF TEAM NICKNAME

The plane never got off the ground, but the nickname certainly did. In the late 1960s, the aircraft company Boeing planned to build a Concorde-style airplane that would travel at a superfast speed. The "Supersonic Transport" would be one of a kind. The plane remained grounded, but the name made a lasting impact on the public. Almost 200 out of the 25,000 contest entries suggested the name SuperSonics.

nba.com FUN FACT

Former guard Dennis Johnson earned NBA Finals MVP honors when he led the SuperSonics to an NBA championship in 1979.

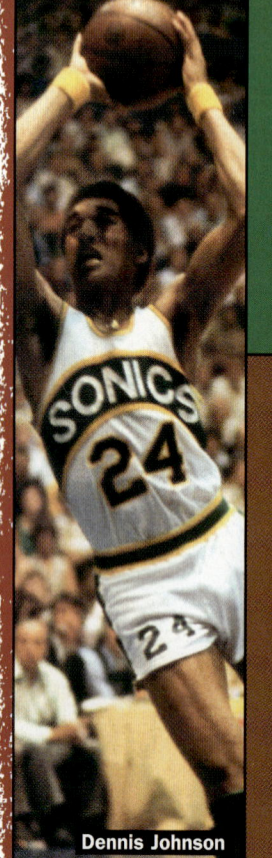

Dennis Johnson

PLAYER TO WATCH: RASHARD LEWIS

Rashard Lewis is an All-Star in the making. The 6-10 small forward has one of the best long-range games in the NBA. Lewis is redefining the word *rain* in the city famous for its weather: He rains three-pointers on opponents. In his fourth season, Lewis should continue to shower opponents with his offensive skills.

PLAYER TO WATCH: GARY PAYTON

Gary Payton only knows one way to play—with all-out intensity. The veteran point guard is an excellent two-way player. He is a tough defender who sticks to his opponents, which earned him the nickname "The Glove." On offense, Payton is fearless when slashing to the basket or draining a three-pointer.

RASHARD LEWIS: Soaring Sonic
Rashard Lewis' Regular-Season Scoring Increases

- 1998–99: 2.4 points per game
- 1999–00: 8.2 points per game
- 2000–01: 14.8 points per game

PAST PERFORMANCE

Season	W–L	Pacific Division	Playoff Finish
1995–96	64–18	1st	Lost in NBA Finals to Chicago (2–4)
1996–97	57–25	1st	Lost in Western Conf. Semifinals to Houston (3–4)
1997–98	61–21	1st (tied)	Lost in Western Conf. Semifinals to L.A. Lakers (1–4)
1998–99	25–25	5th	Did Not Qualify
1999–00	45–37	4th	Lost in First Round to Utah (2–3)
2000–01	44–38	5th	Did Not Qualify

TORONTO RAPTORS

HISTORY OF TEAM NICKNAME

Toronto became the NBA's 28th franchise and the first outside the United States when it originated in 1995. When it came time to select the team's nickname, the prehistoric era influenced the decision. The success of the movie *Jurassic Park*, plus the overall popularity of dinosaurs, made an impact with the local fans in supporting the nickname Raptors.

nba.com FUN FACT

Toronto Head Coach Lenny Wilkens is the NBA's all-time leader in coaching victories. He has 1,226 entering the 2001–02 season. Wilkens also excelled on the court as a nine-time NBA All-Star player.

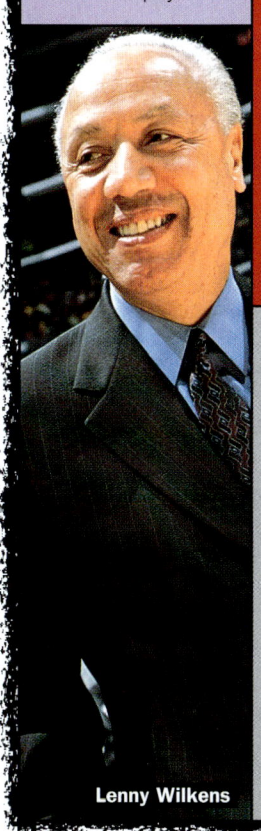

Lenny Wilkens

PLAYER TO WATCH: VINCE CARTER

"Half-Man Half-Amazing" has expanded his game. Instead of jumping over people, Vince Carter is also nailing jumpers. Carter's perimeter game has presented even more problems for defenders. Now instead of just worrying about Vince's dunks, opponents have to worry about getting burned from outside.

PLAYER TO WATCH: MORRIS PETERSON

What can Toronto fans expect from Morris Peterson this season? Mo points, mo rebounds, mo assists and mo highlights. The player they call Mo Pete should excel in his second season with the Raptors. The 6-7 forward-guard plays with tremendous poise and confidence, which is understandable, given his ability to bury jumpers all over the court.

VINCE CARTER: Elevating His Game
Vince Carter's Regular-Season Scoring Increases

- 1998–99: 18.3 points per game
- 1999–00: 25.7 points per game
- 2000–01: 27.6 points per game

PAST PERFORMANCE

Season	W–L	Central Division	Playoff Finish
1995–96	21–61	8th	Did Not Qualify
1996–97	30–52	8th	Did Not Qualify
1997–98	16–66	8th	Did Not Qualify
1998–99	23–27	6th	Did Not Qualify
1999–00	45–37	3rd	Lost in First Round to New York (0–3)
2000–01	47–35	2nd	Lost in Eastern Conf. Semifinals to Philadelphia (3–4)

29

Utah Jazz

HISTORY OF TEAM NICKNAME

New Orleans is the home of jazz. So when the NBA granted a franchise to the city in 1974, it made perfect sense to name the team after the sweet-sounding music. The team kept its name five years later when it moved to the picturesque setting of Salt Lake City, even though the city lacked the musical tradition.

nba.com FUN FACT

A spectacular showman, Pete Maravich led the NBA in scoring during the 1976–77 season, averaging 31.1 points per game.

"Pistol" Pete Maravich

PLAYER TO WATCH: KARL MALONE

Karl Malone is built like a Mack truck. At 6-9, with 256 pounds of chiseled muscle, Malone drives by opponents. At age 38, the Mailman delivers All-Star numbers night in and night out for the Jazz. He's the second-leading scorer in NBA history, with more than 32,000 points.

PLAYER TO WATCH: JOHN STOCKTON

John Stockton is gritty, durable and one of the greatest point guards to ever play the game. The 6-1 point guard is the NBA's all-time leader in assists and steals. Stockton and teammate Karl Malone have formed one of the greatest guard-forward combinations in NBA history.

STOCKTON AND MALONE: PLAYOFF CONSISTENCY

Most Consecutive Seasons in NBA Playoffs

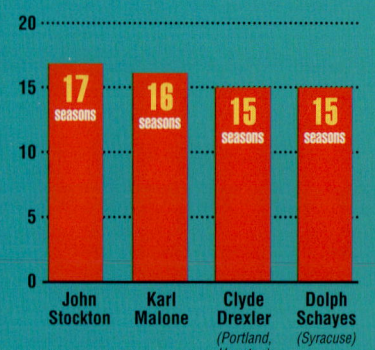

- John Stockton: 17 seasons
- Karl Malone: 16 seasons
- Clyde Drexler (Portland, Houston): 15 seasons
- Dolph Schayes (Syracuse): 15 seasons

PAST PERFORMANCE

Season	W–L	Midwest Division	Playoff Finish
1995–96	55–27	2nd	Lost in Western Conf. Finals to Seattle (3–4)
1996–97	64–18	1st	Lost in NBA Finals to Chicago (2–4)
1997–98	62–20	1st	Lost in NBA Finals to Chicago (2–4)
1998–99	37–13	1st (tied)	Lost in Western Conf. Semifinals to Portland (2–4)
1999–00	55–27	1st	Lost in Western Conf. Semifinals to Portland (1–4)
2000–01	53–29	2nd (tied)	Lost in First Round to Dallas (2–3)

WASHINGTON WIZARDS

HISTORY OF TEAM NICKNAME

What is a Wizard? The name represents a mysterious power, and highlights the wise and magical nature of the team. This nickname follows a long list of names in the franchise's history. The team originated in Chicago in 1961 and was called the Packers before changing its name to Zephyrs. When the team moved to Baltimore in 1963, the name was changed to Bullets, which stuck as they moved to Landover and Washington, D.C., until 1997 when it was changed to Wizards.

nba.com FUN FACT

Wes Unseld became the second player in NBA history to win both Rookie of the Year and MVP honors in the same season. The only other player to accomplish that feat was Wilt Chamberlain of the Philadelphia Warriors.

Wes Unseld

PLAYER TO WATCH: RICHARD HAMILTON

Richard Hamilton doubled his points per game average last season. The Wizards leading scorer averaged 18.1 points per game, doubling his 9.0 average from his rookie season. Hamilton has a scorer's touch and can get his points in a variety of ways. This could be the season he becomes a star.

PLAYER TO WATCH: COURTNEY ALEXANDER

Pay attention to Courtney Alexander this season. The second-year player was one of the NBA's top rookies last season, earning March Rookie of the Month honors. Alexander is a natural scorer who is a threat from the perimeter as well as near the basket.

RICHARD HAMILTON: Monumental Improvement
Richard Hamilton's Regular-Season Point Production

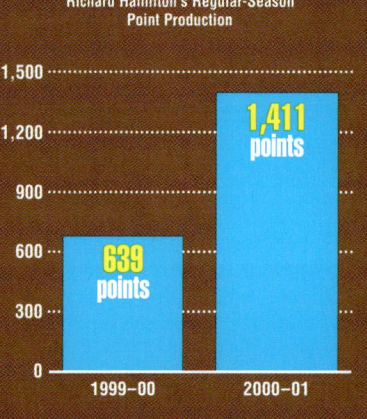

- 1999–00: 639 points
- 2000–01: 1,411 points

PAST PERFORMANCE

Season	W–L	Atlantic Division	Playoff Finish
1995–96	39–43	4th	Did Not Qualify
1996–97	44–38	4th	Lost in First Round to Chicago (0–3)
1997–98	42–40	4th	Did Not Qualify
1998–99	18–32	6th	Did Not Qualify
1999–00	29–53	7th	Did Not Qualify
2000–01	19–63	7th	Did Not Qualify

Your Guide to the NBA Season and NBA Playoffs

Imagine you're a reporter and your assignment is to cover the NBA season and playoffs. Your task is to keep a daily log of wins and losses, as well as determine the winning percentages of all 29 NBA teams. Are you up to the challenge? Sure you are. After all, this book gives you everything you need to complete the job. With the NBA regular-season standings chart, the NBA Playoffs grid and the official NBA Team Tracker marker, following the NBA season has never been so easy.

Simply track the teams throughout the regular season and write in their win/loss records and winning percentages. Whether you're watching the games, logging on to NBA.com for results or checking teams' progress with the sports section of a local newspaper, you can update the records of all of the NBA teams on a day-to-day basis. Simply wipe off the old results on the standings chart and write in the new numbers.

It's that easy! You can keep track of wins and losses as well as a team's winning percentage (wins divided by total games). And when the NBA Playoffs roll around, you have the official NBA grid to track the teams as they battle for the ultimate prize, the NBA championship.

Happy Reporting!